CALICO ILLUSTRATED CLASSICS

Herman Melville's

Moby Dick

ADAPTED BY: Jan Fields

ILLUSTRATED BY: Eric Scott Fisher

magic
wagon

visit us at www.abdopublishing.com

Published by Magic Wagon, a division of the ABDO Group,
8000 West 78th Street, Edina, Minnesota 55439. Copyright
© 2010 by Abdo Consulting Group, Inc. International copyrights
reserved in all countries. All rights reserved. No part of this book
may be reproduced in any form without written permission from
the publisher.

Calico Chapter Books™ is a trademark and logo of Magic Wagon.

Printed in the United States of America, Melrose Park, Illinois
102009
012010

 PRINTED ON RECYCLED PAPER

Original text by Herman Melville
Adapted by Jan Fields
Illustrated by Eric Scott Fisher
Edited by Stephanie Hedlund and Rochelle Baltzer
Cover and interior design by Jaime Martens

Library of Congress Cataloging-in-Publication Data

Fields, Jan.
  Moby Dick / adapted by Jan Fields ; illustrated by Eric Scott Fisher ;
based on the works of Herman Melville.
     p. cm. -- (Calico illustrated classics)
  ISBN 978-1-60270-709-2
  [1. Whaling--Fiction. 2. Whales--Fiction. 3. Sea stories.] I. Fisher,
Eric Scott, ill. II. Melville, Herman, 1819-1891. Moby Dick. III. Title.
  PZ7.F479177Mo 2010
  [Fic]--dc22
                                                    2009033965

Table of Contents

The Spouter Inn

Call me Ishmael. By training, I am a country schoolmaster, but my heart often longs for waves and water. Whenever I find myself growing gloomy and short-tempered, I must take to the sea.

I ship as a sailor. Being ordered about takes some getting used to, but I do it. They pay me, and I very much like to be paid.

Though I had always sailed on merchant ships, I decided to sign on a whaler for a new adventure. So I stuffed a shirt or two into my carpet bag and headed for Massachusetts.

I arrived in New Bedford on a Saturday night, too late to catch the ferry to Nantucket. I wanted a cheap place to stay, and I knew the cheapest lodging would lie in the deepest gloom.

Blocks of blackness lined the streets. Once or twice, I saw a candle move through the night like a ghost in a tomb. Finally, I came to a crooked building where a sign swung on rusty chains. It read "The Spouter Inn: Peter Coffin."

Lodging with a man named "Coffin" must surely be cheap, I thought. I entered the public room and looked around. Whaling lances and harpoons hung on the smoke-stained walls. On the far side, the bar was made from the arched bone of a whale's jaw.

I told the landlord I wanted a room. He said they were full. "But," he added, "if you don't mind sharing, there's room to bunk in with a harpooner staying here."

Since I had no desire to wander in the cold night, I agreed. I ate my meal with other shivering boarders in a room with no fire. We lingered over our scalding tea, warming our frozen fingers on the mugs.

"Landlord," I whispered as the man passed, "which one is the harpooner?"

"Oh, none of these," he said, grinning. "The harpooner is a dark chap. And he eats nothing but rare steak."

Groups of rowdy seamen came and went, but the harpooner was never among them. Finally, I called to the landlord, "What sort of chap keeps such late hours as this harpooner?"

"He's not normally so late," the landlord said. "It must be that he couldn't sell his head."

"Do you mean to say that this harpooner is actually out peddling his head around town?"

The landlord nodded. "I told him not to. The market's flooded."

At this I lost my temper. "I come to your house and want a bed. You tell me you'll give me half a bed but a harpooner fills the other half. Now he's out selling his head. Do you think I would sleep with a madman? Or give money to a trickster?"

"Be easy," the landlord said calmly. "The harpooner just returned from the South Seas. He brought up a lot of shrunken heads from New Zealand."

Why had he not spoken plainly before? The landlord chuckled. "The harpooner's never been this late. He must have found other lodgings. Let me show you the bed."

I followed him to another freezing room with a huge bed. The landlord placed his candle on the old sea chest that served as a table. Then, he bid me good night and left.

A tall harpoon leaned against one wall with a seaman's bag close by. I wasted no more time looking around and tumbled into bed. I had drifted into a light doze when I heard heavy footfalls in the passage. A glimmer of light came from under the door.

The harpooner! I lay perfectly still. The stranger came into the room with a candle in one hand and a shrunken head in the other.

I had just begun to breathe again when the man pulled off his hat. He was bald with only a small knot of hair twisted up on his forehead. The skin of his bald head glowed purplish.

Finally he turned to face me in the glow of the candle. I thought for a moment that the man had been badly beaten because his face was so marked. Then I realized the marks were tattoos.

If he had not been standing between me and the door, I would have run. I considered climbing out the window as the harpooner undressed for bed.

Suddenly, he lurched toward the bed with his tomahawk in hand. "Speak!" he demanded. "Are you a devil here to kill me in the night? I'll kill you first!"

"Help!" I shrieked. "Landlord! Save me!"

"Who are you?" the harpooner demanded again, waving the tomahawk around. At that moment, the landlord burst into the room. I scrambled from the bed and ran to him.

"Don't be afraid," he said. "Queequeg here wouldn't hurt you."

"Look at him!" I shouted. "He threatened me with that tomahawk! What if he made those shrunken heads and wanted mine next?"

This brought a roar of laughter from the landlord. "That's a pipe," he said. "Queequeg likes a bit of a smoke before bed, is all." He turned to Queequeg. "He's rented half the bed, you understand? You came in too late for me to warn you."

"I understand," Queequeg said.

I straightened. "Well, tell him to stash his tomahawk, or pipe, or whatever. I don't want a man smoking in bed with me."

Queequeg agreed. I bade the landlord good night, climbed in bed, and tumbled into a restful sleep.

Breakfast

When I awoke the next morning, I found Queequeg had rolled over in the night and lay with his long arm across me. I tried to push his arm away, but he hugged me tighter in his sleep.

I called out, "Queequeg!" He answered with a snore.

That was really quite enough. I thrashed about. His grip tightened around my neck.

"Queequeg," I squeaked, drumming my heels against the bed. Finally, he drew back and sat suddenly upright, shaking himself awake.

He stared at me, rubbed his eyes, and looked again. Then he jumped out of bed. Speaking in short sentences, he let me know that he would dress quickly and leave me to do the same.

He put on his tall top hat, then grabbed his boots and crawled under the bed. He had such a struggle wrestling into his boots in the tight space! The bed rose into the air several times and then thumped down again.

Finally, he crawled out, pulled on the rest of his clothes, and shaved with the sharp edge of his harpoon. He grabbed his jacket and left the room, carrying his harpoon before him.

I dressed quickly and hurried down to breakfast. The common room was full of shaggy men with the look of the sea about them.

"Grub, ho," the landlord cried as he flung open a door and led us to breakfast. I expected to hear endless whaling stories over each meal, but the men ate as quietly as their collected manners allowed.

After breakfast, I decided to go to church, even though the weather was ghastly. So I wrapped up in my shaggy jacket and fought my way through the storm to Whaleman's Chapel.

The chapel was unique. Like many, the pulpit sat high above the congregation, but no stairs led up to it. Instead, a slide ladder and a pair of red manropes hung down to climb.

Along the wall on either side of the pulpit were marble tablets with black borders. Each tablet was a memorial to a man lost at sea.

I looked around the congregation. It was during this look about that I noticed Queequeg sitting quite near me. Shortly thereafter, Father Mapple seemed to blow in with the storm. He threw off his wet outer garments and climbed the ropes to the pulpit.

Once in the pulpit, he drew up the ropes behind him. Then, he began a lively story about Jonah and his encounter with the whale. After the tale, we were released again into the storm.

Back at the public house, I found Queequeg studying a book with great concentration. As I looked at him, I was struck by what a peaceful man he seemed.

I took a seat near him. We spoke for a moment about our lodgings, then turned to look at the book together. We got on quite well, and I was pleased to see Queequeg grew more talkative as we chatted.

After supper, he even presented me with his embalmed head, which I took to mean that we were now truly friends. Queequeg agreed, we were bonded now and in the traditions of his culture he would die for me if necessary.

Queequeg's Story

That evening, Queequeg spoke of his native island, and I was eager to hear more. He seemed happy to tell me—I think he did not often find anyone interested in hearing his tale.

He came from Kokovoko, an island in the South Pacific that is not shown on any map. He was the son of the ruler of his tribe and would be called on to rule one day. But he longed to see more of the world.

Whalers came and went from the island, seeking food and supplies. Queequeg wanted to travel with them. He hoped to learn secrets that would help his people.

Queequeg approached a whaling captain and asked to join his crew, but the crew was full. Queequeg was not one to give up easily. He lay in wait near where the ship must pass and climbed the side of the ship.

The captain tried to have Queequeg removed, but the young man was strong and stubborn. Finally, the captain gave in and so a king's son became a whaleman.

Through his time with the strangers, Queequeg learned to wear their clothes, talk their talk, and do the job of a harpooner. He feared that his contact with such men had made him unfit to rule his people.

He told me he would look for a ship in need of a harpooner. I told him of my own intent to ship out on a whaler from Nantucket and he quickly agreed to do the same.

The next morning we borrowed a wheelbarrow and carried our things down to the schooner that served as a ferry to Nantucket. We soon had our things stowed aboard the schooner and were on our way.

I was delighted to finally have water carrying me into the wind again. But some of the crew began jeering and mocking Queequeg and me for being such clear friends.

Finally one of the foolish young men slipped behind Queequeg, mocking him. Queequeg spun around, grabbed the young man, and turned him quite upside down. He tossed him in the air, then spun him and set him down again on his feet.

"Captain!" the young man bellowed as he ran to the officers.

"What do you mean by such tossing?" the captain shouted at Queequeg. "You might have killed the young man."

Queequeg turned to me as if he didn't speak a word of English. I pointed to the silly, quivering young man and with great sweeping motions, pretended to communicate how close the man had come to death.

"That fish too small to kill," Queequeg said, laughing. "I only kill big fish."

"No more of your tricks here," the captain roared. While he railed at Queequeg, a strain on the mainsail suddenly sent the boom swinging wildly. Queequeg's tormentor was swept overboard by the boom.

The boom swung so wildly, the crew hardly dared try to stop it. Queequeg dropped to his knees and let the boom sail past him. He then crawled under it, fashioned a lasso, and flung it over the swinging boom. He wrestled it into submission.

While the crew hurried to repair the damage, Queequeg dove over the side of the ship. When he hit, he looked around the freezing waves for the young man who had been swept overboard.

Queequeg dove beneath the waves. Moments later, up he popped with the young man in tow. They were pulled safely aboard the boat. After that, no more fun was made of Queequeg.

Nantucket

Peter Coffin had recommended we stay in Nantucket at the inn of his cousin. *The Try Pots* was the inn's name as it only served chowder for breakfast, dinner, and supper.

When we first arrived at the inn, I stared at its odd signpost. It looked more than a little like a gallows. I shook off this idea, for I was a man of reason.

When dawn rose over Nantucket, I expected to go with Queequeg to find a whaling ship for us. But, he insisted that Yojo had sent him a vision that he should stay at the inn and pray while I chose our ship.

Now, Yojo was a small carving of an odd hunchbacked figure that Queequeg carried in his bag. Each evening, he would rest it in the ashes of the fireplace and pray. By this I guessed Yojo to be a god of some sort. Since I had no experience at all in whaling ships, Yojo's vision seemed unwise to me. But Queequeg was certain, so off I went.

Three whaling ships were signing crew. I chose the *Pequod* and quickly boarded it. On deck, a brawny old man sat inside an odd kind of whalebone tent.

"Are you captain of the *Pequod?*" I asked.

"What do you want with the captain?" he asked.

"I was thinking of shipping."

"Do you know anything about whaling?"

"No, though I expect I can learn," I said.

The man stared at me for long moments. "The captain of this ship has but one leg," he answered. "The other was chewed up and swallowed by the most monstrous whale in the sea. That's what whaling is. Do you still want to go?"

"I do, sir."

Bildad took me below decks to meet his partner, Peleg. The two partners argued at length about my pay, which would be a portion of the profit from the journey. I was offered less than I'd hoped, but I had long ago given up thoughts of growing rich from my voyages.

"I have a friend who wants to ship, too," I said. "He has killed more whales than I can count. Shall I bring him tomorrow?"

"Bring him," the partners agreed.

Before I left, I asked if I'd be able to meet the captain.

"You'll not meet him before you sail," Peleg said. "But I can assure you, Captain Ahab's a good captain. An odd man and a bit moody, but a good captain. He has a fine wife and a child. He's just been a bit strange since the whale chewed off his leg. It'll pass."

The Ship

The next day, Queequeg and I set off to the ship so he could sign his papers. As Queequeg boarded, Peleg stared at him suspiciously.

"Tell me," he bellowed as if suspecting Queequeg's tattoos may have rendered him deaf, "have you ever stood in the head of a whaleboat? Did you ever strike a fish?"

Queequeg jumped into the bows of one of the whaleboats hanging on the side of the *Pequod* and cried, "Do you see the small drop of tar on the water there? Suppose him be the eye of a whale."

Then taking sharp aim, he threw his harpoon and stuck the glistening tar spot out of sight.

"Now that whale is dead," Queequeg announced.

After this, Queequeg's papers were produced and signed. Directly after leaving the *Pequod*, we heard a cry down the dock, "Shipmates, have ye shipped in her?"

"You mean the *Pequod*?" I asked.

"Aye," the strange, tattered man said, throwing his whole arm out to point. "That ship there."

"Yes," I said. "We have just signed the papers to ship out."

"Did they say anything about your souls?"

I stared at him, realizing he might be more than just tattered. "Queequeg," I said softly, "let's go. This fellow has broken loose from somewhere."

"Stop!" he cried. "Did they tell you about your captain?"

"I've heard that he's a good whaler," I said, "and a good captain to his crew."

Then the strange man began to babble about Captain Ahab, but he spoke in such fits and starts that none of it made sense. I grew annoyed and insisted we knew all we needed to about the captain.

"Who are you to be muttering about the captain?" I demanded. "What's your name?"

"Elijah," he said simply. And at that, we parted company. I must admit, the man left me uneasy, since he carried the name of an ancient prophet. But I would give no more attention to the rambling of a crazy man.

The next two days passed in great activity as the ship was loaded. Because we would be at sea for three years with no grocers or doctors handy, we had to pack heavy. During these days, Queequeg and I did not once see Captain Ahab, though I asked about him often. I was assured he was expected soon.

Finally the day for boarding came, and we hurried to the ship in the misty dawn. I spotted the dim outline of men running ahead of us.

"Look!" I said to Queequeg. "We'll not be the first aboard today."

Just as we reached the ship, Elijah appeared again babbling about the ship and the strange shadowy sailors. I wanted nothing more to do with him.

"Never mind him," I said.

Queequeg and I stepped aboard and found everything silent. We looked around but found only empty spaces or locked ones.

"Where could those sailors have gone?" I asked Queequeg.

But Queequeg only shrugged, and I wondered if he had seen them at all. As the sun rose, the crew came on board in twos and threes and everyone set to work.

Everyone except Captain Ahab, who remained hidden in his cabin.

Ahab

Having sailed on many merchant vessels, I knew captains often kept to their cabin until well away from port. Steering the ship out to sea was done by the pilot. Peleg and Bildad had that chore well in hand, calling out commands with vigor.

Finally the time came for them to return to the dock. Peleg and Bildad said their good-byes.

"I hope ye'll have fine weather now," Bildad said. "Captain Ahab will soon be moving among ye. A pleasant sun is all he needs. Be careful in the hunt, mates."

They dropped into their small boat and headed away. Then with the night breeze blowing, the *Pequod* plunged like fate into the Atlantic.

The chief mate of the *Pequod* was Starbuck. He was a long, earnest man, though his time at sea seemed to have made him superstitious. He believed strongly in being cautious.

"I'll have no man in my boat," said Starbuck, "who is not afraid of a whale." He believed an utterly fearless man would be a danger to himself and his mates.

"Aye," said Stubb, the second mate. "Starbuck is as careful a man as you'll find anywhere." Stubb was good-humored, and given to singing even in the face of the most dreadful danger.

The third mate was Flask, a short, stout fellow. He behaved as though each whale had dealt him a dreadful insult.

Starbuck, Stubb, and Flask commanded the actual whaleboats that battled the whales. Each man chose a harpooner for his boat. Starbuck selected Queequeg.

Stubb's harpooner was a member of a tribe from Martha's Vineyard. He had an amazing throwing arm, though he could not match Queequeg in sheer size and strength.

The third harpooner was born much farther away on African soil. He was a gigantic man with coal black skin. He had joined a whaler for much the same reasons as Queequeg. He stood so tall over Flask that they looked like a king and pawn on a chessboard.

It might seem strange to picture men so different shipping out together, but such was often the case on whalers. Skill, strength, and courage are the traits that build the brotherhood of whalers.

For several days after leaving Nantucket, I met most of the crew of the *Pequod*, but still had not caught a glimpse of our captain. With each day that passed without sight of Captain Ahab, Elijah's ranting dug deeper into me.

Finally, on a gray and gloomy morning, not long after Christmas, I mounted to the deck and glanced around. Captain Ahab stood upon the quarterdeck.

He stood so tall and still that he seemed cast from bronze. A thin white scar ran from his gray hairs into the neck of his clothing. No one knew the story behind the scar.

I was so stunned by the sight of the captain that I didn't immediately notice the carved and polished ivory peg that replaced his leg.

Standing so motionless while perched on a peg seemed impossible. Then I spotted a hole in the quarterdeck. In this hole, the bone leg was steadied.

The captain didn't speak, only stared out as still as death. After a time, he withdrew again to his cabin.

Each gloomy day as we traveled toward warmer seas, he would spend time silently standing in this hole or seated on an ivory stool. Finally, he walked heavily for a bit on the deck.

A Mystery

As the sky grew less gloomy, Ahab came out more and more. Though he said so little, he might have been a ghost were he not so solid.

When the *Pequod* sailed into the bright tropical spring, Captain Ahab grew more restless. He slept little and paced the night-cloaked deck. The *thump-thump* of his pacing woke us many a night.

One night, Second Mate Stubb spoke to the captain lightly. He suggested if the captain must walk the planks at night maybe something could be wrapped around the ivory.

Captain Ahab spun around and roared that he would not be muffled aboard his own ship. Ahab stalked toward the second mate and said,

"Be gone or I'll clear the world of thee!"

Though not cowardly, Stubb dashed back toward the cabin. "Is he mad?" he muttered.

Some days after, Ahab was pacing the decks after breakfast. He stopped suddenly and called to Starbuck, "Send everybody aft!"

"Sir?" Starbuck replied.

"Send everybody aft," Ahab repeated. When the ship's company was assembled, Ahab turned to the men with a serious tone. "What do ye do when ye see a whale, men?"

"Sing out for him!" we shouted together.

"Good!" the captain said, looking wildly pleased. "And what do ye do next, men?"

"Lower away and go after him!"

Again Ahab seemed fiercely glad. The captain held up a coin. "Do ye see this Spanish doubloon?" He carried the coin to the mainmast and held it against the wood. "Whosoever raises the cry for a white-headed whale, he shall have this ounce of gold, my boys!"

The men cheered as Captain Ahab nailed the doubloon to the mast. Then the harpooner Tashtego stepped up, "That whale sounds like the one some call Moby Dick."

"He is," Ahab said. "Do you know him?"

"Does he sweep the water with his great tail before he goes down?" the harpooner asked.

"And does he have a curious spout?" Daggoo threw in. "Very bushy and mighty quick?"

"And does he have a good many irons in his hide?" Queequeg cried. "All twisted like . . ." and there his English failed him and he screwed his hand round and round.

"A corkscrew," Ahab said. "Aye, Moby Dick bears many failed harpoons. And his spout is a big one like a whole shock of wheat. And he fan-tails. It is Moby Dick ye have seen, men!"

"Captain," Starbuck called, less eager than the rest, "is it not Moby Dick that took thy leg?"

"Aye!" Ahab shouted with a terrific animal sob. "It was. And I'll chase him to my death before I give him up! Are you with me men?"

"Aye, aye!" shouted the seamen.

"Bless ye," he seemed to half sob and half shout. "And are you not game, Mr. Starbuck?"

"Game enough if we find him as we go about our business," Starbuck said. "But I came to hunt whales, not my commander's revenge."

Ahab gestured across the eager men and said, "Who could oppose my cause without rebellion?"

I shouted with the crew. My oath rose with theirs.

Now, the sea breeds superstition, myths, and tales. And many were the tales of Moby Dick. But I knew that behind great myths were great acts. Behind fear lie monsters. And if only the smallest of the tales of the White Whale were true, they were true enough for all.

No more was discussed of our captain's call for the White Whale in the days ahead. For another mystery had caught the attention of the crew.

Since early on, it was whispered that something drew Captain Ahab to the hold each night. Crewmen heard odd sounds where no man ought to be—rustlings, scrapings, even a cough. Something more than stores lay in the hold, and the crew grew anxious to know when that something would be revealed.

The First Lowering

Ahab knew that chasing only the one whale would not long please the crew. A voyage without profit would send them to complain to Starbuck. Thus, he called often to the three mastheads and reminded them to keep a bright lookout.

On a whaling ship, three mastheads are kept manned from sunrise to sunset. In the tropics, this is a pleasant task. You stand a hundred feet above the decks, striding along the deep as if the masts were gigantic stilts.

I kept guard poorly as I am a dreamer. And indeed, I was not on the mast when the first whale was spotted.

It was a cloudy, hot afternoon, and the seamen lazed about the decks. We started when we heard the call. High aloft in the crosstrees, Tashtego stretched his hand out like a wand.

"There she blows!" he bellowed. "There! About two miles off. It's a school of three."

Instantly everyone leaped to their tasks. We raced to prepare the three whaleboats. Soon they hung over the sea while each of us who would board stood ready.

Then, a sudden exclamation took every eye from the whale. All glared at Ahab, who stood surrounded by five phantoms freshly formed out of air. We saw what had been hidden in the holds—men.

This strange group of men flitted on the other side of the deck, casting loose a boat that swung there. We had thought it a spare boat, as all whale ships carry many spares.

A new harpooner now stood by its bows. He was tall and dark with a single white tooth that stuck out from his thin lips. He wore his long, snow-white hair braided and wound around his head to make a turban. The four rowers had the tawny skin that showed they were from the Manilas.

"All ready there, Fedallah?" Ahab cried to the white-turbaned harpooner.

"Ready," the man half-hissed.

"Lower away then!" Ahab shouted across the deck. "Lower away I say!"

At his thundering command, our three boats dropped into the sea while the sailors leaped down the ship's side into the boats below.

The rowers set to work. No sooner had we pulled out when a fourth keel came up. In this ship, the five strangers rowed while Ahab stood stern. He hailed Starbuck, Stubb, and Flask to spread widely.

Thus we began the hunt. Each of the commanders of the individual boats led differently. Stubb sighed at his crew, "Pull, pull, my fine hearts-alive."

Starbuck commanded in an intense whisper. "Seethe her, seethe her, my lads."

And Flask cried, "I can't see three seas off." Daggoo flung Flask high upon his shoulders.

Starbuck pulled across Stubb's bow. With the two boats very near each other, Stubb called out, "What think ye of these unexpected whalemen, sir?"

"Smuggled onboard before we sailed," Starbuck responded, never taking his eyes from the water ahead. "A sad business, Mr. Stubb, but let all your crew pull strong. Duty and profit hand in hand."

"Aye, aye," Stubb agreed. At least one layer of the mystery was solved.

"Queequeg, stand up," Starbuck commanded in a fierce whisper.

My friend sprang nimbly up and directed eager eyes toward the sea. Then we heard Tashtego, Stubb's harpooner, cry, "There they be!" All four boats launched in pursuit of one troubled spot of water.

"Pull, pull, my good boys," Starbuck commanded. We rushed along with the rising wind.

"There is time to kill a whale yet before the squall comes," Starbuck whispered. Then came an enormous groan. "That's his hump. Give it to him!" our commander said.

Queequeg's harpoon whooshed. Then a mighty push from behind slammed us, while the front of the boat seemed to strike on a ledge.

A gush of scalding vapor shot up near us. Something rolled like an earthquake under us and the whole crew was tossed into the sea.

The whale had been merely grazed by the harpoon, and it escaped.

The Spirit Spout

Though nearly swamped, the boat was basically unharmed. We swam around, collected the floating oars, and tumbled back into our place.

The wind howled and waves dashed us where they would. The squall roared and crackled around us like a wildfire.

We hailed the other boats, but could neither see them nor hear them. Starbuck relit the lantern and hung it on a pole that he handed to Queequeg. Queequeg held it high, hoping to be spotted.

Drenched and shivering, we waited through the night and into the thin dawn's light. Mist still spread over the sea. We heard a faint creaking. The sound came nearer until a form appeared through the mist. The *Pequod* loomed into view, bearing down upon us.

We dove from the boat and the hull of the *Pequod* rolled over it. But we had been spotted and the crew hauled us aboard the ship.

"Queequeg, does this sort of thing often happen?" I asked when they had dragged me, the last man, to the deck. He said it did.

"Mr. Stubb," I said, turning to the man as I shook myself, "did you not say Mr. Starbuck is the most careful and prudent of whalemen? Do you call chasing a whale into a foggy squall careful?"

"I've chased whales in a leaking ship through a gale," he said.

I turned to Flask then, seeking to find a sane man aboard. But he also felt what we had gone through was minor. I could see only one option.

"Come along," I called to Queequeg. "I have need of a witness. It's time to write my will afresh."

When the will was done and I felt more myself, I came upon Flask and Stubb in earnest discussion. Stubb marveled at Ahab's desire to take to a whaleboat with but one leg. But Flask felt Ahab had leg enough for the hunt.

It gave me pause to think though. The owners of the *Pequod* had not meant for Ahab to lead a whaleboat. This must be why he brought aboard his own rowers and harpooner in secret.

With time, the strange rowers began to blend in with the rest of the crew. The hair-turbaned Fedallah remained a mystery. He seemed uninterested in socializing and his strange looks were off-putting.

As we sailed deeper into our journey, Fedallah took to keeping a mainmast watch at night. Night watches were not the norm aboard a whaler. Though herds of whales are seen by night, not one whaleman in a hundred would go after them.

Still, one calm and moonlit night, Fedallah called out, "There she blows!"

Walking the deck with quick, side-lunging strides, Ahab commanded the sails set in pursuit. Though the ship sped swiftly, and every eye peered like eagles, the silvery jet was no more seen that night.

This midnight spout returned some nights later to the same effect. In fact, it returned so many nights that eventually talk turned to superstition.

The spout was surely none but Moby Dick, beckoning us on. The monster was trying to lure us to death in the most remote and dangerous seas.

Squid

Whenever two whale ships come together, the captains normally seek a meeting, called a gam. The captain of one ship rows over to the other. The first mate of the opposite ship rows over to the first. Thus an exchange is made of crewmembers, mail, and stories of the ship's encounters.

Not far south of the Cape of Good Hope, we came across our first whaler since departing. The ship was the *Goney*, which means "albatross." It was clear the *Goney* had been long upon their voyage. The hull of the ship was bleached white while its sides ran with streaks of rust like dried blood.

The *Pequod* and the *Goney* passed close. A hail went up from our quarterdeck, "Ship ahoy! Have ye seen the White Whale?"

The captain of the *Goney* leaned over the side of his ship with a bullhorn to his mouth. But then, the horn tumbled from his hands and into the sea. The rising wind drowned out his words.

Captain Ahab looked across but made no call for a boat. "Up helm," he cried instead. "Keep her off round the world!"

Not many days after passing the *Goney*, we came upon another homeward-bound whaler named the *Town-Ho*. This time a gam was called, for the *Town-Ho* had news of Moby Dick.

We learned the ship had launched against the White Whale. The ship's mate, Radney, had commanded the boat that reached the creature first.

Radney told the men to beach the boat on the whale's back. Then the harpooner would drive his lance into the creature to set anchor.

The bowman hauled them up and up through the blinding foam. Suddenly the boat struck against something and keeled over. The mate spilled out and tumbled into the sea next to the whale.

Radney struck out swimming to remove himself from the eye of Moby Dick. But the whale rushed around in a sudden storm of motion. It seized Radney between his jaws, reared high in the air, and then plunged headlong down.

As the whale dived, the rope that bound it to the boat jerked the boat downward also. The bowman quickly cut the line and the whale was free. At some distance, Moby Dick rose again with tatters of Radney's red shirt caught in its teeth.

After the meeting with the *Town-Ho*, we steered northeastward. We entered a meadow of brit, the yellow substance right whales feed upon.

On the second day after that, we spotted the whales themselves. The huge black forms of the slow creatures looked like lifeless masses of rock. As they offered nothing we wanted, we sailed past.

Suddenly Daggoo called out from his place on the main masthead. He had spotted a great white mass lazily rising in the water until it gleamed before our prow.

"There!" Daggoo bellowed. "There she breaches! The White Whale!"

Ahab cast eager eyes in the direction of Daggoo's outstretched arm. When he too spotted the white mass, he gave orders for lowering.

The four boats raced toward their prey. The white mass went down and we waited its return with oars suspended. Lo, in the same spot where it sank, once more it slowly rose.

The mass floated on the water. Long arms radiated from its cream-colored center. They curled and twisted like a nest of snakes.

With a low sucking sound, it sank again. "What was it, sir?" Flask called to Starbuck.

"A giant squid," Starbuck said in his fierce whisper. "And some say few whaling ships return to their ports after seeing one."

Ahab said nothing, only turning his boat and sailing back to the *Pequod*. The rest of us silently followed.

Stubb's Supper

Queequeg declared the squid a good omen. "When you see the squid," he said as he sharpened his harpoon, "you quick see the sperm whale after him. The whale, they eat squid." Queequeg's words were soon proven true.

The next day, I stood my turn at the front masthead. I swayed to and fro in the heat. Suddenly, a gigantic sperm whale rolled in the water. Its skin was glossy black in the sun's rays.

"Clear away the boats!" Ahab cried. Before the boats were down, the whale calmly swam to the side of the ship.

"Hold your oars," Ahab commanded. "Speak in whispers."

Thus we glided in chase. Suddenly, the monster flitted his tail forty feet in the air and sank out of sight like a tower swallowed up.

"There go flukes!" sailors cried from each of the whaleboats. And we stopped and waited.

The whale rose again, just in front of Stubb's boat. We threw aside silence as the whale raced away.

"Start her, my men!" Stubbs cried. "Give me the long stroke, Tashtego." And the oarsmen dug deep to a racing pace.

"Woo-hood, washer!" screamed Tashtego.

"Knee-deep! Knee-deep!" yelled Daggoo.

"Ka-la! Koo-look!" howled Queequeg.

With this chorus of wild yells, our keels cut the sea. The oarsmen pulled and strained with all they had. Finally Stubb shouted, "Stand up, Tashtego! Give it to him!"

The harpoon flew straight and true.

"Stern all!" Something went hissing along every one of the oarsmen's wrists. It was the whale rope following the harpoon's line in the racing whale. Soon the boat flew through the boiling water. Each man aboard clung to his seat.

"Haul in!" Stubb cried. All hands began pulling at once to draw the boat closer to the whale.

Stubb threw dart after dart into the whale. A red tide poured from its sides until it rolled in blood. The whale's spout blew jet after jet. Finally, the whale began to weaken.

"Pull up!" Stubb called. The boat came along the whale's side. Stubb plunged his lance into the whale, seeking its heart. The creature fought, thrashed, and died.

Stubb's whale lay some distance from the *Pequod*, so the three boats towed it back to the ship. Though eighteen men rowed with all their strength, progress was slow.

Darkness came on, but the *Pequod's* lights guided our way. Heavy chains were dragged along the ship's deck and thrust out the portholes to be fastened to the whale's body.

Finally tied by the head to the stern and by the tail to the bows, the whale pressed close to the *Pequod*.

Upon our return, Stubb strutted around the decks. "Daggoo," he commanded, "go and cut me a steak from the whale. I'll have a steak before I sleep."

The ship's cook was awakened and fixed Stubb's steak with plenty of grumbling. Finally at midnight, Stubb stood on deck and ate his whale steak by the light of the sperm oil lanterns.

In the waters beside the *Pequod*, thousands of sharks also dined on the dead whale. Sharks can reduce a whale to little more than a skeleton in six hours. So when the sharks move in, an eye is kept on them.

Queequeg and another seaman decided the number of sharks required action. They lowered three lanterns and the two mariners darted at the sharks with long whaling spades.

These razor-sharp tools stuck deep into the skulls of the sharks, killing them. Again and again the men struck at the sharks. Soon, the bloody water caused the sharks to strike at one another as much as at the whale.

The next morning, we set to the task of butchering the whale. The first thing that must be done is the beheading. This is no small matter as the whale's head takes up much of its body. Still for all the difficulties, it took but ten minutes for Stubb to behead the sperm whale.

The head is then held at the front of the ship until the body is stripped. To begin the strip, Starbuck and Stubb put a hook just above the nearest of the whale's two side fins.

Setting the hook itself is always done by a harpooner. This task fell to Queequeg with me as his second. Queequeg and I were joined together by the monkey-rope. My job was to stay aboard the *Pequod* and prevent Queequeg from slipping off the carcass.

Though I trusted Queequeg completely, he was massive and the whale was slippery. I was not at all certain I would last out the day.

Finally, the hook was set and the next step could begin. The crew began hauling the hook line using a massive pulley system. As they hauled on the rope, the entire ship leaned over on its side. At last, with a *snap* the ship rolled away from the whale.

The rope rose, dragging the first strip of blubber. As the men heaved, the blubber was stripped off the whale like peel from an orange. The blubber of a very large sperm whale will yield nearly a hundred barrels of oil. These strips were hauled, cut, and lowered into the blubber room in the ship.

When we had stripped the whale, we cut the corpse loose to drift behind us. Immediately birds and sharks fell upon the mass and fed.

At this point, the men went below to dine and rest. Ahab walked the decks alone, watched over only by the three men on the

masthead. Suddenly a masthead voice called out, "Sail ho!"

"Aye," replied Ahab, his voice as light as any had heard it. "Where away?"

"Three points on the starboard bow, sir."

By and by, the mastheads showed the stranger to be a whaler. Each ship of the American whale fleet has a private signal to show other whalers which ship they see.

The *Pequod* set her signal as did the other whaler, which proved to be the *Jeroboam* of Nantucket.

The Jeroboam's Story

The *Jeroboam* changed her course and lowered a boat. A side ladder was rigged on the *Pequod* so that Captain Mayhew could visit. But the strange captain waved it away. The *Jeroboam* had sickness onboard and he would not risk infecting the *Pequod*'s crew.

The sea was blustery. Sudden swells often swept the smaller boat past. The rowers then had to haul the small whaleboat back to our side again.

Along with oarsmen and captain, the boat carried a small, crazy-looking man. Stubb took one look at him and cried, "That's him!" He had heard tales of this stranger from the crew of the *Town-Ho*. This was the lunatic who claimed to be the archangel Gabriel.

This young man had convinced Mayhew's crew that he had some mystical power. When the captain realized Gabriel's presence was disruptive, he decided to drop him off at the first opportunity. But Gabriel convinced the crew that they would die if they removed him. Now, he even claimed to control the sickness.

"I fear not thy sickness, man," Ahab called from the bulwarks. "Come aboard."

Gabriel jumped to his feet in the small boat. "Think of the fevers! Beware of the plague!"

"Gabriel!" cried Captain Mayhew. "Thou must either—" But a wave shot the boat far ahead and the rest of the captain's words were lost to us.

"Hast thou seen the White Whale?" Ahab demanded when the two crafts were again side by side.

"Think of thy whaleboat," moaned Gabriel. "Broken and sunk! Beware the horrible tail!"

Captain Mayhew again tried to calm the crazed man. When again we rested side by side, Captain Mayhew said they had indeed encountered Moby Dick and he shared the tale.

Early on, Gabriel had insisted that the *Jeroboam* must not hunt the White Whale. Moby Dick was a god, he said, and would destroy them all. His ranting dampened most of the crew's enthusiasm.

Still, a year or two into the voyage the watch sighted the White Whale. The chief mate Macey convinced five men to man his boat. As Macey began his pursuit, Gabriel climbed to the masthead and yelled his visions of doom into the wind.

Finally, Macey's boat grew close and he stood to throw the harpoon. At that moment, a broad, white tail rose from the sea. It struck the mate, throwing him in a long arc into the sea. After this horrible event, Gabriel's place as prophet was sealed aboard the *Jeroboam*.

At the end of his tale, Captain Mayhew asked if Ahab intended to hunt the White Whale himself. As soon as Ahab acknowledged that he was, Gabriel launched into a ranting fury.

Through the rant, Ahab turned aside from the young man, offering no reaction or comment.

"Captain," he said when it was over, "I believe I have mail for some in your crew."

Starbuck was sent to hunt through the mailbag that was sent with each outgoing ship on the chance of connecting with other ships and passing letters. The letter proved to be for the mate Macey.

"Oh, poor fellow," Mayhew said. "Let me have it."

Starbuck tried to pass it down but again the wind worked against them. The letter ended up in the hands of Gabriel. Gabriel struck it through with a boat knife and cast it back aboard the *Pequod*.

"Nay, keep it thyself," he cried. "You'll be going his way soon enough."

Then Gabriel demanded they row back to the *Jeroboam*. The small craft quickly shot away from the *Pequod*.

The Tap

Now, as sometimes happens, the head of the sperm whale hung alongside the *Pequod* for quite some time. This caused the ship to sail with a decided lean.

It was at this time that we caught sight again of right whales. Ahab ordered that a right whale should be killed if opportunity offered.

The whaleboats led by Stubb and Flask were sent after the whales at first spout. Pulling farther and farther away, the whaleboats were soon almost invisible to the men at the masthead.

Then suddenly, the boats raced back toward the *Pequod*. The whale that towed the boats seemed intent on hurling himself against our hull. At the last instant it dove under the keel. The two whaleboats split and hurtled alongside the ship.

We felt a swift tremor as the strained line scraped beneath us. Then the whale rose once more. Stubb and Flask struck at the whale again and again with their lances. Finally the whale turned upon its back and died, leaving Flask and Stubb with the job of towing the whale to the *Pequod*.

"What does the old man want with this lump of foul lard?" Stubb said.

"It's a charm," Flask replied. "Once a ship has a sperm whale's head hoisted on one side and a right whale's head on the other at the same time, that ship can never capsize."

Stubb snorted. "Who says such a thing?"

"Fedallah," Flask said. "He's full of charms."

"Fedallah is the devil in disguise," Stubb muttered. "The reason we've not seen his forked tail is because he keeps it coiled in his pocket."

"So what does the old man want with the devil?" Flask asked.

"A deal," Stubb said. "I've heard the devil will make a deal for your soul or something of that sort."

"If he's the devil, you might take care," Flask cautioned. "He might take it in his head to drown you."

"I should like to see him try," Stubb ranted as he hauled up into the *Pequod*.

With a great head on each side, the ship now had an even keel. But, it was sorely strained from the great weight. Thankfully, we did not need to bear it for long.

A sperm whale's head contains the richest prize of the sea. It holds the case, the great cavern filled with 500 gallons of pure spermaceti, a type of oil.

The case fills the entire top of the whale's head. Sperm whales have nearly one-third of their length taken up by head. This means a case can be twenty-six feet deep when it is hoisted up lengthwise to be tapped.

On the morning of the tap, Tashtego ran straight out upon the mainyard arm. He carried a whip block to hoist buckets of spermaceti from the vast well within the head.

Tashtego secured the whip block to the mainyard arm. Then, he tossed one end of the block's rope to a man on deck to tie on the first bucket. He used the other end of the rope to scramble down onto the head.

Someone handed Tashtego a short-handled spade to cut into the whale's head. The stout bucket attached to the whip rope was hoisted to Tashtego. He inserted a pole into the lowered bucket to guide it into the hole he'd made.

He gave a sign and the bucket raised, full to bubbling. The bucket was caught up on deck and emptied into a large tub. A second bucket was lowered to Tashtego and filled.

As the buckets scooped out more and more of the spermaceti, Tashtego had to thrust deeper and deeper. After nearly twenty bucket dips, Tashtego slipped on the waxy skin and dropped headfirst into the whale's great case.

"Man overboard!" cried Daggoo. He called for a bucket and used it to be lowered onto the whale's head. But Tashtego had fallen too deeply to reach. Meanwhile, the head trembled and jerked upon its hooks as Tashtego fought to escape.

The combined weight of the two harpooners and the thrashing was too much for the whale's flesh. One of the two enormous hooks tore out and the head tipped to the water, making the *Pequod* reel and shake.

With a boom, the last hook ripped through and the head plunged into the sea. Daggoo clung to the hanging whip rope, but Tashtego was sinking with the head.

Hardly had the blinding sea spray cleared away than Queequeg dove over with a boarding sword in hand. Everyone fell silent as we watched the empty sea.

"Ha!" cried Daggoo as an arm thrust forth from the water. "It is both!"

And then we saw it—Queequeg boldly swimming with one hand while the other clutched the long hair of Tashtego. A waiting boat was lowered and both men were loaded into it.

The Jungfrau

We continued our hunt and eventually spotted another whaling ship, the *Jungfrau* from Germany. It launched a boat to row to us well before the ship had grown close. Then we spotted the captain standing impatiently in the bows with a lamp-feeder in his hands.

"He's out of oil," Flask cried in disgust. For a whaling ship to need oil for its lights suggested a sorry bit of whaling.

As the German captain mounted the deck, Ahab abruptly questioned him about Moby Dick. But Captain Derick admitted his ship had not captured a single whale and was truly inexperienced.

The captain's cans were filled and Derick departed. But he was barely launched when the cry was raised from the mastheads of both vessels. Whales!

Derick did not return to his ship but immediately struck out after the whales. He had a slight lead on us and a strong lead on the rest of his crew. We spotted an ancient bull swimming slowly behind the pod.

Derick's boat still led the race to the whale. The German turned frequently to grin back at us and wave his lamp-feeder.

"The man has no manners," Stubb declared. "Pull now, that graybeard is ours."

Our boats grew close to the German. Derick called his harpooner to strike, hoping to get the first iron into the whale and thus claim it. His harpooner stood, preparing a throw.

Queequeg, Tashtego, and Daggoo all sprang up and threw their barbs over the head of the German harpooner. All three struck and we raced ahead, towed by the whale's headlong rush. We bumped the German boat aside with such force that both Derick and his harpooner spilled out.

"Don't worry," Stubb cried as his boat shot past. "You'll not wait long for pickup. I saw some sharks, and they'll be along to help you."

The elderly whale's run was short, and his death quick. As soon as the whale died, he began to sink and the three whaleboats held him up as we waited on the ship.

We cut quickly into the whale's flesh to secure it to the small boats. We found the entire length of a corroded harpoon imbedded in its flesh. More astonishing still, we found a lance-head of stone that the flesh had grown completely over it.

Who had darted that stone lance? Perhaps Northwest Indians had long before America was discovered. As the whale was lashed to the *Pequod*, it renewed its determination to sink.

The ship was dragged as though the whale's body grew heavier with each passing second. The chains on the whale were under such strain we could not cast them off.

Stubb bellowed, "Cut the big chains!"

Queequeg seized the carpenter's hatchet. "Aye, aye." He slashed at the largest fluke chain, sending a shower of sparks into the sea. With a terrific snap, the ship righted and the whale sank.

As the carcass sank, a watcher from the masthead spotted the *Jungfrau* lowering her boats to chase a finback. Unskilled whalers sometimes confuse the spout of the finback for the sperm whale.

I wondered how long it would be before Derick would be hunting oil from another real whaler.

CHAPTER 15

A Purse

Within days of our encounter with the *Jungfrau*, we replaced the lost carcass with another. We dealt quickly with the blubber and spermaceti and sailed on for the Straits of Sunda, which lie between Sumatra and Java.

Though these straits have a bloody history of pirate raids, we plunged through with our hearts set on the whales often found there. We nearly reached the open sea without a sighting. Suddenly the cry was raised. We gazed upon a pod of whales.

The whales must have sensed us for they rushed to reach the open water. The *Pequod* pressed upon them. The harpooners gripped their weapons and cheered.

Suddenly, Tashtego was heard, loudly directing attention to something in our wake. Leveling his glass, Ahab revolved in his pivot-hole and cried. "Pirates and they are after us!"

Ahab paced the deck, looking first to the whales and then to the bloodthirsty pirates. If the wind held, we could catch the one and outrun the other.

After steadily dropping the pirates, the *Pequod* shot into the open sea. The whales seemed to be tiring. The ship grew near. Then the wind died away and word was passed to spring the boats.

As the boats hit the water, the whales rallied again and formed close ranks. Still we pulled and pulled for several hours. Suddenly the compact columns of whales broke up. Our boats immediately separated, each making for a lone whale at the edge of the group.

Queequeg flung his harpoon. The wounded whale dragged us straight for the heart of the herd. Queequeg steered us through the panicked whales, sheering off from one then edging away from another. Starbuck stood in the bows, lance in hand, pricking out of our way whatever whales he could reach.

Our towing whale pulled us into a clearing at the center of the herd. At this, he jerked the harpoon out and vanished. So dense was the wall of whales around us that we could see no exit.

In the center of the herd, cows and calves were sheltered. The calves snuggled right up to our gunwales and touched the boat itself. Queequeg patted their foreheads. Starbuck scratched lightly at their backs with his lance. But no one caused harm to the calves for we would not survive a panic so deep in the herd.

Suddenly, the peace at the center was broken as a wounded whale charged through the line. This whale had tangled himself in a harpoon rope tied to a cutting-spade. The spade had worked its way from the whale's flesh and now

hung at the end of the rope, dashing itself against his fellow whales as he passed.

"Oars," Starbuck whispered. He and Queequeg traded places so Starbuck could be at the helm. "Pull! Scrape their backs if you must but pull!"

The boat was now all but jammed between two huge black backs and was sure to be crushed. By desperate work, we shot into a temporary opening. After many similar narrow escapes, we made it to the outside of the herd.

As the whales rushed away from us, we saw that Flask had killed one. In the end, his catch was all we had to show of our adventure, but that is the way of whaling. The more whales, the less capture sometimes.

⚜️

A week or two later, we sailed slowly over a midday sea. An unpleasant smell was in with the breeze. Presently we spotted a French whaler holding two whales.

By the smell, any oil recovered from the rotting creatures would be bad. As we grew closer, we saw one whale had grown thin and dry of oil before it died.

"That French ship is easily pleased," Stubb scoffed, then grew thoughtful. "Though that dry whale may contain something of greater value than oil." With that he hastened away to the quarterdeck to speak to the captain.

We grew close to the French ship and the stench lay upon us thickly. Stubb called for his boat's crew to row for a talk with the stranger.

Stubb called out to ask if any had seen a white sperm whale. The chief mate called that he had never even heard of such a whale. Stubb then asked the chief mate how he felt about his smelly task of harvesting useless whales.

"The captain will not believe they are useless. He listens to no one here. Come aboard, perhaps he will listen to you."

Stubb was soon aboard and plotting with the chief mate. The mate acted as Stubb's interpreter. He used the opportunity to tell the captain that plague was associated with whales.

The captain instantly rushed forward and commanded his crew to cast the whales loose. Stubb offered to tow the dry whale away to lessen the chance of plague. The captain agreed and Stubb returned to his boat.

As Stubb helpfully towed the old whale, the French ship rushed away. The *Pequod* slid between the French ship and Stubb.

Then Stubb pulled up to the rotting body. He cut into the whale, a little behind the side fin. The stench at this cut made all the previous smell seem almost pleasant. Stubb dug deeper and deeper.

Suddenly from the very heart of the horrible smell, a faint perfume seeped to our noses.

"I have it!" Stubb yelled with delight. "A purse!"

He thrust both hands into the whale's side and drew out handfuls of something that looked like soap or richly mottled cheese. It was soft enough to dent with your thumbs and bore a color between yellow and ash.

This was ambergris, worth a gold quince an ounce. Some six handfuls were drawn out before Ahab demanded that Stubb return to the *Pequod* or be left behind.

Leg and Arm

"Ship ahoy! Hast ye seen the White Whale?" Ahab cried when next we spotted a ship showing English colors. Ahab's ivory leg was in plain view.

"See you this?" the strange captain asked, raising his arm. It was carved of whalebone with a wooden head like a mallet in place of a hand.

"Man my boat!" cried Ahab. He rushed to the side of the English ship. The English captain quickly lowered a massive blubber hook to Ahab's ship. The captain slid his thigh into the curve of the hook. He rode up with all the comfort of a boy cradled on the branch of an apple tree.

When Ahab came within reach, the strange captain reached up his ivory arm for Ahab to shake. Ahab thrust out his own ivory leg and they crossed ivory.

Ahab cried, "Let us shake bones together. Where did thou see the White Whale? He took that arm off, did he?" Ahab asked as he slid from the hook to stand beside the captain.

"Aye," the captain said. His ship had lowered to chase a pod of whales and the English captain's own whaleboat fastened on one of them. The beast pulled them round and round until suddenly a great white head breached.

"Harpoons stuck out near his starboard fin," the Englishman said.

"They were my irons!" Ahab bellowed.

"This old great-grandfather with the white head ran into the pod and snapped at my fast line."

Moby Dick had caught the line in his teeth. When the Englishman's crew tried to draw in the line, they found themselves bouncing off the White Whale's hide. At the same time, the whale they had fastened swam free.

The captain had snatched a harpoon and let the whale have it. The harpoon caught the mass of iron and ropes in the whale, but it quickly worked free.

Moby Dick dove. At this dive, a flapping iron caught the captain in the shoulder. It dragged through his flesh to his wrist before coming clear.

The wicked wound grew black with infection. The ship's doctor had cut off the captain's arm to save his life.

"What became of the White Whale?" Ahab demanded.

"We didn't see him again for some time," the one-armed captain said.

"Didst thou cross his wake again?"

"Twice."

"But could not fasten?"

"Didn't want to try to," the Englishman said. "Isn't one limb enough?"

Ahab nodded. "But he will still be hunted. How long since thou saw'st him last? Which way was he heading?"

"East, I think," the Englishman answered, drawing back from Ahab's intensity.

Ahab lurched back to the side of the ship. "Man the boats."

The other captain stared, then turned toward Fedallah and whispered, "Is your captain crazy?"

But Fedallah put a finger on his lips and slid over the side to take the whaleboat's steering oar. Ahab swung into the boat. He landed with such energy upon his whaleboat that his ivory leg received a half-splintering shock.

Once aboard the *Pequod*, it took a bit of time for Ahab's temper to cool. It cost his leg still another crack when he twisted in his pivot-hole to roar a command at the steersman. The ivory received such a wrench that Ahab did not deem it entirely trustworthy and demanded the carpenter make him another.

CHAPTER 17

The Whale Watch

Aboard any whaler, the hold is flushed with sea water each day to swell the wood of the whale oil barrels and prevent leaks. One day as the water was pumped back out of the hold, oil rode upon the water.

Starbuck went down to the captain's cabin to report this crisis. He found Ahab with charts stretched before him. At the sound of Starbuck's footsteps, Ahab called out, "Begone!"

"The oil in the hold is leaking, sir," Starbuck said, addressing the back of the captain's head. "We must stop and find the source."

"Heave to and tinker with a parcel of old hoops?" the captain asked.

"We spill more oil in one day than we may

make in a year. What we came 20,000 miles to get is worth saving, sir."

"*If* we get it. Begone. Let it leak. I'll not stop now."

"What will the owners say, sir?"

"The owners are not captain of this ship," Ahab roared. He seized a loaded musket from the rack and pointed it toward Starbuck. "Begone!"

Starbuck grew red in the face, then visibly calmed himself. "Aye, Captain. But I warn ye. Let Ahab beware Ahab."

Ahab stared after Starbuck's retreating back and put the gun back in the rack. He walked away muttering, "Ahab beware Ahab, there's something to that."

Ahab raised his voice to the crew. "Furl the t'gallant-sails. Break out in the main hold and find your leak."

The search for the leak was no small chore. Barrel after barrel was hauled to the deck and found sound. It was during this work that

Queequeg caught a chill. The chill soon became a fever. He grew too weak to do anything but lie in his hammock. Not a man on the crew believed he would survive.

Finally Queequeg made a request. He did not want to be tossed in the sea as was the tradition. He wanted a wooden coffin cast into the sea like a boat. This was more like his own people's customs.

The carpenter was called to measure Queequeg and build his coffin. When it was

finished, Queequeg tested the fit. For several minutes, he lay quietly in his coffin. Then, we hauled him out and put him back in his hammock. There, he began the surprising process of getting better.

I was glad of my friend's recovery and delighted to see him change his coffin into a sea chest. In the days ahead, he spent many hours carving copies of his own odd tattoos into the wood. He said the symbols were filled with magic.

When we emerged at last upon the great South Seas, the blacksmith set up his forge upon the deck. He filled his days with repairs to metal tools and edges.

One day Ahab approached the forge, shaking a bag that rattled like gold coins. "I want a harpoon made," he said, "from these nail stubs of the shoes of racing horses."

"Captain Ahab," the blacksmith said, "you have the best stuff we blacksmiths ever work."

"I know it, old man. It will weld together to form a harpoon that will stick in a whale like his own fin bone."

And so the blacksmith set to the task. Ahab called for twelve rods to be made and twisted into the shaft of the harpoon. He watched the creation of each rod, even stepping in to weld the twelve into one himself.

As Ahab labored over the fire, Fedallah crept by. He bowed his head toward the fire as if saying a blessing. When Ahab looked up, he slid away.

The creation of the new harpoon deepened the darkness upon the captain. A few weeks later, we came upon another whaling ship, the *Bachelor*. It was returning to Nantucket with more oil than any whaler could hope to gather in a single voyage.

We could see the men of the *Bachelor* dancing and laughing. The captain of the ship stood serenely on the ship's quarterdeck.

Ahab too stood on his quarterdeck, shaggy and black. He had vowed at the creation of his harpoon to shave no more until he'd killed the White Whale.

"Hast thou seen the White Whale?" Ahab demanded.

"No, though I've heard of it," the other answered. "I don't believe in him at all."

"Thou art a fool. Sail on!" Ahab watched the ship pass cheerily along.

The sighting of the lucky *Bachelor* seemed to shed luck upon us. The next day, whales were seen and four were slain—one of them by Ahab.

With so many slain, it was impossible for the *Pequod* to watch over all through the night. The whale on the windward side was watched over by the boat that killed it. That boat was Ahab's. The crew dozed until the tap of sharks' tails on the light planks woke Ahab.

"I have dreamed it again," he whispered.

"Of the hearses?" Fedallah asked. "You'll have neither hearse nor coffin."

"Yes," Ahab agreed moodily. "There are no hearses for those who die at sea."

"Before you die," Fedallah replied, "you will see two hearses on the sea. The first will not have been made by mortal hands. The wood of the second must be grown in America."

"A strange sight that would be," Ahab said with a dark laugh. "And when will you die?"

The strange man shrugged. "Before you."

"Then you think Moby Dick will not kill me?" Ahab asked.

"Only hemp can kill you," Fedallah said.

Ahab shook his head. Surely Fedallah did not think Ahab would be hung some day? "Then I shall live forever."

Fedallah had no answer to that, and both men rode silently for the rest of the night.

CHAPTER
18

The Doubloon

As we neared the equator, the crew cast eager eyes toward the doubloon more and more often.

Ahab clumped out on deck with the ship's quadrant to sight for latitude. Suddenly Ahab flung the instrument from him.

"Curse thee, quadrant," he swore. "You show me where we are, but not where we must be." The old man then trampled the instrument.

Not long after this, the Japanese sea turned against us, as tropical seas often do. The worst of all storms, the typhoon, burst from a cloudless sky and rode down upon us.

The *Pequod* was battered and rocked by the rain, the sea, and the wind. The sky roared with thunder and blazed with lightning. A great rolling wave dashed high up against the ship's side and into the bottom of Ahab's whaleboat.

Lightning struck close to the ship. Starbuck cried for the rods to be raised above the masts to draw away any strikes.

"Avast," cried Ahab, waving the men away. "Let's play fair here. Give the storm its chance."

"Look!" Starbuck shouted, pointing. The three tall masts burned silently at their tips like candles.

Stubb roared with laughter at the sight. "That masthead flame signals good luck, for those masts are rooted in the hold that is full of sperm oil. Do you see?"

"Aye," cried Ahab. "The white flame lights the way to the White Whale!"

Starbuck cried, "Look at thy boat, old man."

Ahab's harpoon remained firmly lashed to his broken boat and from the keen steel came a leveled flame of pale, forked fire.

Starbuck grasped Ahab by the arm. "'Tis the serpent's tongue. God is against thee and this ill voyage. Let us make a fair wind of it homeward while we can."

But Ahab pulled away and snatched up the burning harpoon. He waved it like a torch among the crew. "All your oaths to hunt the White Whale are as binding as mine." Then with one breath, he blew out the flame.

In time, the gale died down. Starbuck paced and muttered along the rail. And though Starbuck seemed to be wrestling with an angel, he turned no hand against Ahab that night.

The next morning dawned bright and clear. Ahab stood on his deck, puffed full of confidence in the face of surviving so fierce a storm. He turned to the helm, shouting for the ship's heading.

"East-sou-east, sir," said the frightened steersman.

"Thou liest," the captain roared. "We cannot head east in the morning with the sun astern!"

Then Ahab caught a glimpse of the compasses. Without question, the two compasses pointed east.

The old man barked a laugh. "Last night's storm has turned our compasses."

Ahab called to the crew for the smallest of the sailmaker's needles. "Men, the thunder turned our needles, but I can make one of my own that will point true."

Ahab placed a blunted needle endwise on top of the steel head of a lance. He hammered it several times. Then, he called for linen thread. He suspended the needle, and the steel went round and round then settled in its place.

He shouted, "The sun is east and the compass swears by it."

The *Pequod* continued on her path toward the equator. When the ship finally neared the fishing ground, the night watch was startled by a mournful cry from the darkness.

By morning, stories had already sprung up. It was the cry of the doomed or the dead. It was sirens beckoning the men. It was mermaids wailing for lovers.

Ahab laughed at all the fanciful notions. The cries were seals, he explained. But sailors are superstitious about seals, and they saw no good omen in this.

Later, at change of morning watch, a sailor climbed the masthead, slipped, and fell. A cry was heard as he plunged into the blue sea.

The life buoy was dropped from the stern. When it hit the waves, it filled with water and followed the sailor to the bottom of the sea. This drowning was said to have been caused by the cries of the seals.

The buoy had to be replaced. Queequeg suggested his coffin would serve well. Starbuck said, "There's nothing else for it. Have the carpenter rig it so it is worthy of the job."

And so the coffin was nailed and sealed and set in place.

CHAPTER 19

The Rachel

The next day, a large ship bore down upon the *Pequod*. At the time, the *Pequod* was making good speed through the water. But when the *Rachel* got near, the sails fell as if life had fallen away from them.

"Hast thou seen the White Whale?" Ahab called.

"Aye, yesterday," the *Rachel*'s captain answered. "Have ye seen a whaleboat adrift?"

Ahab said no. The other captain came aboard the *Pequod* and Ahab met him.

"Where was he? How was it?" Ahab demanded.

On the late afternoon of the previous day, the *Rachel*'s boats had chased a group of whales some miles. As the whaleboats grew close, the White Whale suddenly loomed.

The reserve boat was sent after Moby Dick, for it was swiftest. It fastened upon the whale, which towed the boat away from the other three whaleboats.

The *Rachel* gathered the three boats, then turned in search of the last. Though they searched all night, not a glimpse of the missing boat was seen.

The captain asked Ahab to join them in the search. "My own boy is among them," the captain cried, growing more desperate. "I beg you. I will gladly pay you. You must!"

Ahab refused. He commanded the crew that they would not join in. Then he went below to avoid the captain's cries.

The strange captain hurried back to the *Rachel* and returned to the search. The *Pequod* rushed ahead toward Moby Dick.

As Ahab grew stranger, there came changes in Fedallah. The peculiar man was never seen to sleep. He always glided around the deck shuddering and growing thinner each day.

Often Ahab stood on deck and stared at Fedallah even as the strange man stared at him. It was hard to say who seemed more unearthly, Captain Ahab with his gnarled dark beard and fire-burned eyes or Fedallah with his serpent's tooth and turban of hair.

Ahab began to keep his own watch for the White Whale. "I will have the first sight of the whale myself," he said. He rigged a nest of bowlines and used it to raise himself aloft to the main masthead.

Through darker and darker omens we followed a mild wind. A lull can make men edgy or restore them to rest. For Ahab, it made him thoughtful as he stumped up to stand beside Starbuck at the rail.

"Oh, Starbuck," he said, "your eyes are the magic glass. I see my wife and child in thy eye." He sighed a shuddering breath. "Starbuck, stay on board when I pursue Moby Dick. Keep safe the faraway home I see in thy eyes."

"Oh, my captain!" Starbuck cried. "Let us fly these deadly waters! Let us home to our wives and children."

But Ahab averted his glance. He would not turn from his vow though it be his death. He crossed the deck to gaze over the other side but saw two wild faces reflected in the water. Fedallah leaned silently on the same rail.

The Chase

That night, Ahab suddenly sniffed the air and declared that a whale was nearby. He paced until daybreak then yelled, "Call all hands!"

Daggoo roused the crew by pounding on the deck. The men quickly appeared.

Ahab bellowed, "There she blows! A hump like a snow hill. It's Moby Dick! Fate has decreed I raise the White Whale first," Ahab babbled. "Stand by three boats. Mr. Starbuck, stay on board and keep the ship."

Soon all the boats but Starbuck's were dropped. All the boat sails were set, and all the paddles rowed with rippling swiftness.

The whaleboats sped silently through the sea. As they neared Moby Dick, the ocean grew smooth. The whale moved serenely. And from his back hung the shattered pole of a recent lance. Birds lighted upon it now and again.

Then the whale sounded and vanished. The three whaleboats floated, awaiting Moby Dick's reappearance. Within the hour, the breeze freshened, the sea began to swell, and the white birds flew toward Ahab's boat.

Ahab looked far over the side and saw a white living spot. It grew and grew until it turned and plainly revealed two long crooked rows of white teeth floating up from the darkness. It was Moby Dick with mouth wide open.

The glittering mouth yawned and took the bows of Ahab's boat full in its mouth. The inside of the jaw was within six inches of Ahab's head and reached still higher than that. The oarsmen threw themselves to the rear of the boat.

Ahab seethed at being helpless. He seized the jaw in his naked hands to wrench his boat

free. The jaw slipped from him. The whale bit the boat completely in half and the men were thrown hard upon the water.

The whale circled the swimming men. Suddenly the *Pequod* bore down upon them and drove off the whale.

Stubb hauled Ahab into his boat. "Is my harpoon safe?" the old man gasped. "Any missing men?"

"All here."

"Then let us set after him," Ahab roared, coming again to himself. But Moby Dick surged forth and Stubb's boat could not equal the power of the whale.

The *Pequod* drew all aboard so that we might continue the chase. We followed until the night grew too dark to see. And so the first day of the chase was over.

On the dawning of the second day, the *Pequod* raced over the sea to catch up with the White Whale.

Ahab called to be raised to his watchpost. He had barely reached his place when Moby Dick burst into view.

The whale breached, surging from the depths until his entire body hovered in the air. "There she breaches!" the crew yelled.

"Breach your last to the sun, Moby Dick," Ahab bellowed. "Thy hour and thy harpoon are at hand."

Again he called for the boats to be lowered and for Starbuck to stay aboard. The White Whale rushed among the boats with open jaws and a lashing tail.

With his rage, the whale entangled the three harpoon lines in a thousand different ways. The snarled lines drew the whaleboats toward the planted irons. Contact with the bristling barbs and the points of the irons would sink them as fast at the teeth of the whale. Ahab had no choice but to cut them loose.

That instant, the White Whale rushed among the remaining lines. Its flukes dashed

Stubb's and Flask's whaleboats together. Then Moby Dick dove, leaving shattered pieces of boats to circle the waters.

Suddenly Ahab's undamaged boat seemed to leap upward toward heaven. The White Whale shot up, dashed its head against the boat's bottom, and sent it turning over and over in the air.

Now the whale turned and swam leeward away. As before, the *Pequod* swooped in to pick up the men and the bits of boat that could be saved.

When Ahab was hauled to the deck, he leaned heavily on Starbuck's shoulder. All could see his ivory leg had been snapped off, leaving one short, sharp splinter.

The Third Day

"Which way?" Ahab cried as he leaned on Starbuck.

"Dead to leeward, sir."

The captain looked around in alarm at the men who had been pulled from the ocean. Ahab yelped. "Quick, call them all."

But all stood before him—Fedallah was not there. "I saw him dragged under," Stubb said.

"So he is gone before me," Ahab muttered. "It's twisted us for two days," Ahab said. "But tomorrow will be the third. He'll rise once more to spout his last."

And so the *Pequod* chased the whale until dark. The carpenter made Ahab a new leg to face the new day of the chase.

The morning was fair and fresh. Ahab called for sightings before dawn. But into noon, no sightings came.

Suddenly Ahab commanded the ship be turned around. "He's chasing me now," he bellowed. "About! We'll meet him soon."

Then, some points off the weather bow, Ahab saw the spout again. "Forehead to forehead I meet thee, Moby Dick."

The boats were lowered again. In this third rush, I was to replace Fedallah in Ahab's boat. As the captain was lowered, he called for a pause. "Starbuck! Shake hands with me, man."

Their hands met. Their eyes fastened and in Starbuck's hung glittering tears. "Oh, my captain, my captain, go not."

Ahab tossed the mate's arm from him and commanded, "Lower away! Stand by the crew."

The boats moved not far from the *Pequod*. Suddenly the waters around us swelled in broad circles. A vast form shot lengthwise from the sea, trailing ropes, harpoons, and lances.

The whaleboats rushed forward to the attack. But Moby Dick churned its tail among the boats, flailing them apart. Then, it slammed its tail down to smash in the bows from the mates' boats.

Again the *Pequod* collected the men from the broken boats, leaving only Ahab's craft in the water. The White Whale turned to swim away again.

Ahab's boat flew swiftly, propelled by sail and oar. As the *Pequod* and the whaleboat chased, it seemed that Moby Dick must be tiring. Ahab called the men to pick up their pace, but their efforts had attracted a few sharks who struck at the oars. The blades grew jagged and crunched.

"Heed them not," Ahab commanded. "'Tis better rest to strike a shark's jaw than the yielding water."

Moby Dick seemed to care little for Ahab's advance. The whale's side struck the boat, and three of the oarsmen were flung out. Two scrambled back in while the third was left when the whale towed the boat.

Again, Moby Dick ran. Suddenly, he seemed to hear the rush of the *Pequod* after him. The whale turned and bore down upon the ship.

"My ship!" Ahab yelled. The oarsmen strained to pull them toward the rushing whale, but they could not match its speed.

The crew of the *Pequod* saw the whale coming at them. The solid white forehead hit the ship's starboard bow. Then, they heard the waters pour.

"The ship," Ahab moaned. "The second hearse made from American wood."

The whale dove beneath the settling ship and rose again within yards of Ahab's whaleboat. Ahab stood again and darted. The whale flew forward.

The harpoon line ran through the groove, then fouled. Ahab bent to clear it and the flying line caught him round the neck. He was dragged from the boat before the crew knew he was gone.

By then, the whaleboat was pulled by the great sucking of the *Pequod*'s sinking. Caught in the circles, it was pulled out of sight.

Only one man survived the wreck. It was I, Ishmael, who was thrown from Ahab's ship and left behind. I was well away from the destruction that followed. I alone was so far away I was not pulled in with my fellows.

As I swam, the coffin life buoy suddenly shot lengthwise up from the sea. It fell over and floated by my side.

Buoyed up by the coffin for almost a day and a night, I floated. The sharks paid me no interest.

On the second day, I was picked up by the *Rachel*. It was still searching for her missing children, but ended up rescuing another orphan instead.